My Secret Angel and Me

How the Gift of Christmas Came to Be

Created by Ashley Adorno and Rachel Hernandez

Written by Rachel Hernandez – Illustrated by Ashley Adorno

Scripture taken from New International Version. Grand Rapids: Zondervan, 1986

Published in Atlanta, Georgia by For the King Press

My Secret Angel and Me: How the Gift of Christmas Came to Be

ISBN 13: 978-0-615-49480-7

Second Edition 2012

For bulk order prices contact
rachel@mysecretangelandme.com or ashley@mysecretangelandme.com

For more information and updates inquiries visit
www.mysecretangelandme.com

Dedication

This book is especially written for our little angels, Bella, Tyler, Ayla and Cecelia.

To all the children of the world! May you each come to know Christ as your Savior and friend!

To our guardian angels here on earth, Pam Sheldon, Ann Platz, Cecelia McNorrill and Trudy Engebretson. We praise God for your friendship, guidance, love and support!

To our amazing parents, loving husbands and all of our brothers and sisters. Thank you for your unconditional love and encouragement throughout this book and always.

To our angels in Heaven, Kelly Sue Adorno and Joshua Alexander Adorno. Forever missed. Never forgotten.

Down from the sky and through the clouds I flew.

Across the stars I sailed with a message just for you.

So please listen carefully as you hear what I proclaim:

Since I am here from Heaven, I have no earthly name.

Please give me a name so I can start my mission from above.

I have a Christmas secret that will fill your heart with love.

Please think of a name quickly. It's so easy if you try.

Then I'll be yours forever, and we will never say good-bye.

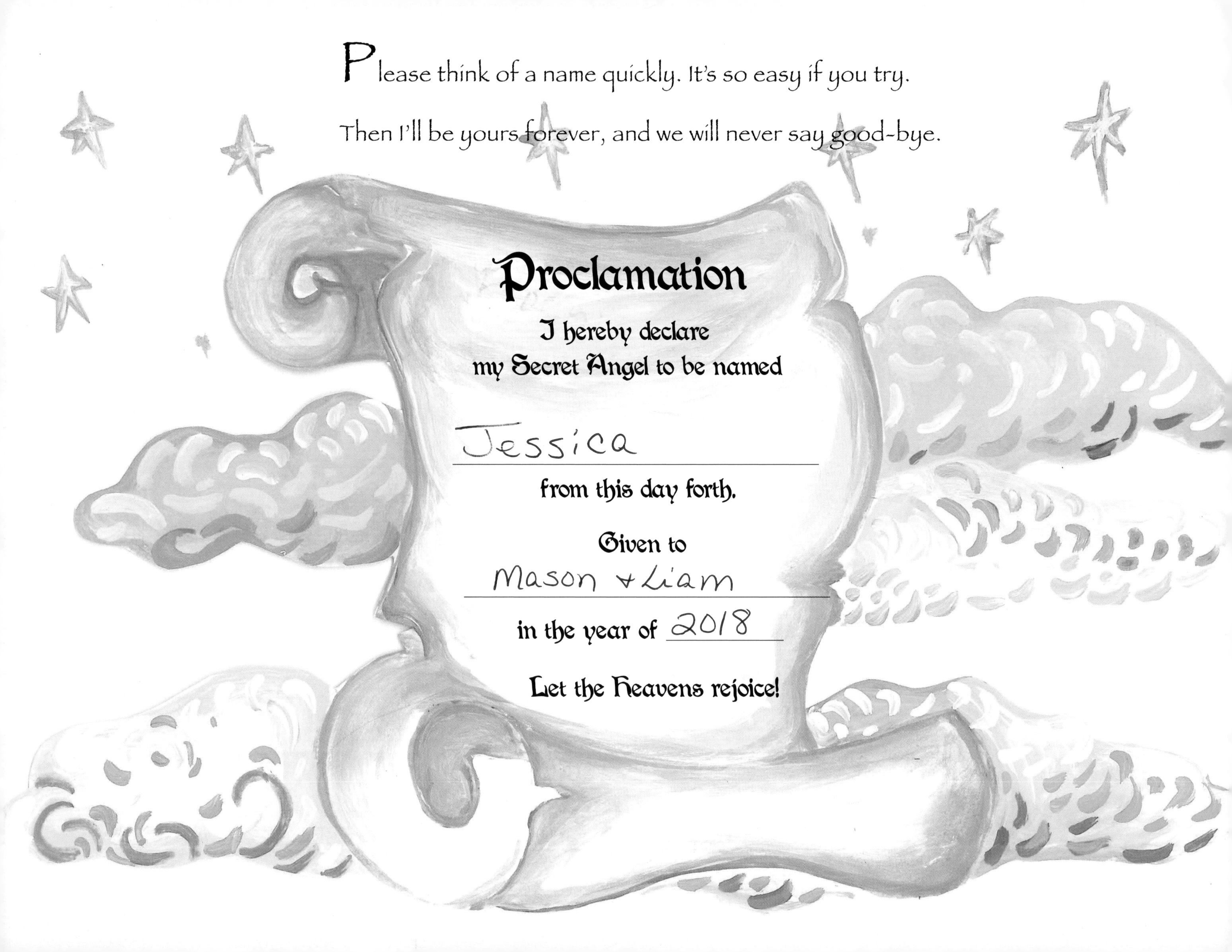

This name has brought me magic! Now I'll always be your guide.

Climb aboard my feathery wings. We're going for a ride!

Back in time we travel.
It's two thousand years ago.

See the angel sitting there
with Mary down below?

I'm sure they see us too;
Its so hard to hide my glow!

The angel said Mary's baby would one day be our King.

But not the kind with lots of gold who wears a diamond ring.

The people didn't need a king with riches or shiny jewels.

They needed a king to teach them God's important rules.

Angel Gabriel said to Mary, "Please don't be afraid.
My message is from God." So she listened and obeyed.

"God picked you to be the mommy of His one and only Son.
So, Mary, name Him Jesus. He's the chosen One."

Mary was engaged to Joseph and wondered, "How could this be true?"

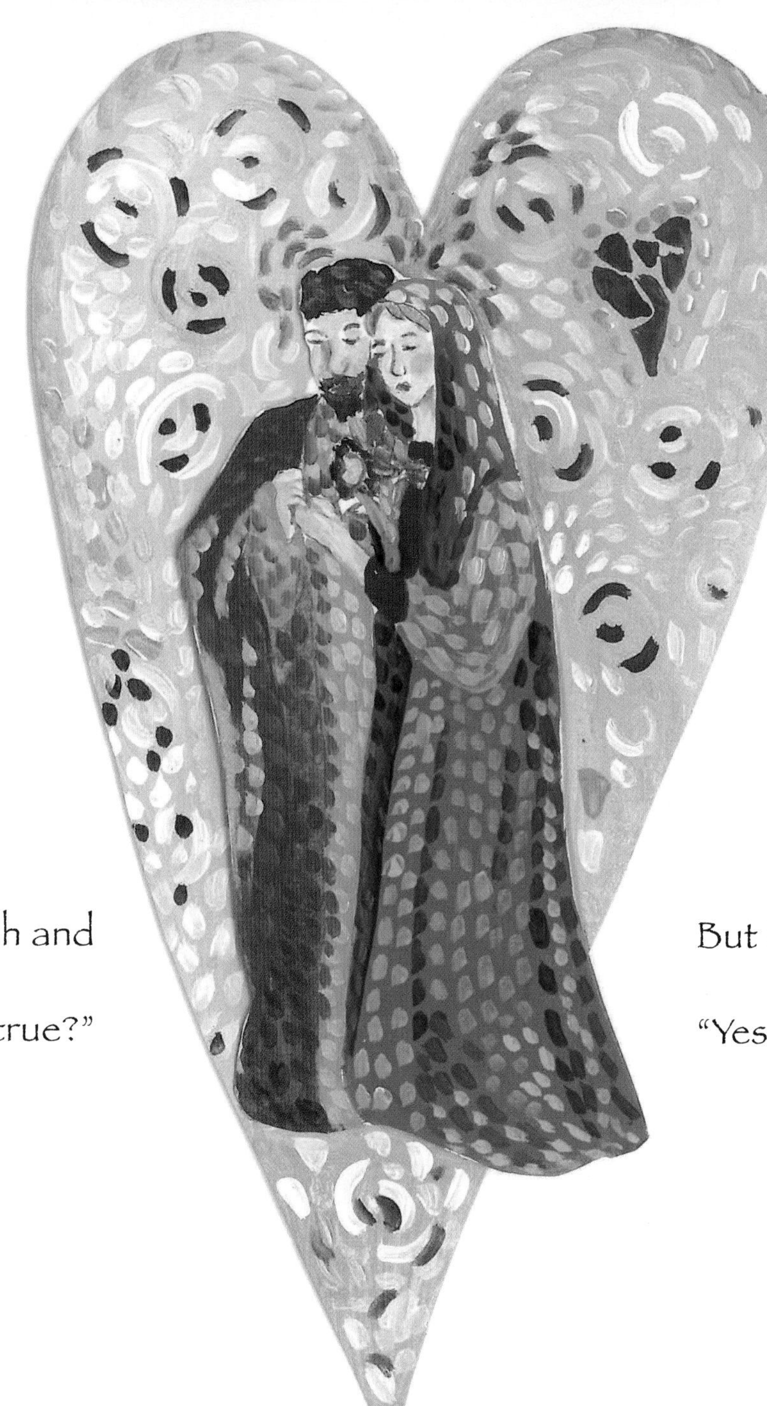

But Mary trusted God and said, "Yes I will do this for you."

And late one night while sleeping,
an angel did appear.
He brought God's words to Joseph
to make it very clear.

"Please care for baby Jesus
and take Mary as your wife.
This Son is like no other,
My gift to all will be His life."

When the day for Jesus' birth was finally close at hand,

Mary and Joseph traveled to a place called Bethlehem.

Christmas was coming so all the angels began to sing!

Rejoicing in the birth of what would be a newborn King!

Mary and Joseph were tired and needed a place to sleep.

But the only place they found was a stable filled with sheep.

It was there that Mary gave birth to baby Jesus on Christmas Day!

The very King of the world was born in a manger full of hay!

"This is the day that the Lord has made; let us Rejoice and be glad in it."
Psalm 118:29

The angels told the shepherds that our King was born at last!

They could hardly believe the news, and they went to meet Him fast!

A bright star lit the sky to help the shepherds find their way.

It also led the Three Wise Men to the stable where Jesus lay.

They gathered all around Him and praised His day of birth.

The very God of Heaven was now a baby here on earth!

Jesus said, ... "I am the light of the world" John 8:12

The Wise Men brought gifts to thank
God for sending Jesus from above.

These gifts made God so happy,
since they gave them out of love!

We can all remember Jesus

in this very same way when

we give gifts to celebrate

His birth on Christmas Day!

Santa thinks of Jesus as he piles presents on his sleigh.

Before he leaves the North Pole, he gets on his knees to pray.

He knows the true gift of Christmas is our Savior from above,

And knows no gift upon his sleigh is greater than God's love.

It's OK to ask Santa if you want a special toy.
But God gives the best gifts of peace, love and joy!

Now you know my secret, and you must believe it's true.
God is the one who tells Santa what he needs to do!

His plan for all of us- even Santa on his sleigh-
is to know that Jesus' birth is the real gift of Christmas Day!

joy
patience
peace
goodness
gentleness
kindness
love

Each night as you sleep, I return to the stars in the sky.

I meet with other angels to tell them how hard you try.

"For he will command his angels concerning you to guard you in all your ways."
Psalm 91:11

I know you want to be good.
It's how God created you to be.
That's why I'm here from Heaven
to remind you of His plea.

God wants you to love others
and always act your best.

Be kind to your friends;
be nicer than the rest.

Remember what I've said,
and behave if you can.

But know God always loves you.
He's your biggest fan!

And each night as you sleep,
my magic will take place.

I'll get a twinkle in my eye,
And then I'll move my face.

And when my wings start to flutter,
I'll take off at a fast pace!

Before you wake up, I'll be back to hear you snore.
I'll move to a different place than I did the night before.

You might not see me hiding. I'm in a secret spot.
I hope you'll try and find me. I like this game a lot!

But, please don't move me.

I'm right where God wants me to be.

I fly to different places in your

house so I can see.

It's now time for you to sleep.
Our story has come to an end.

I must return to Heaven.
I have good news about you to send.

Please look for me again tomorrow.

Love,

Jessica
____
your secret angel and friend.

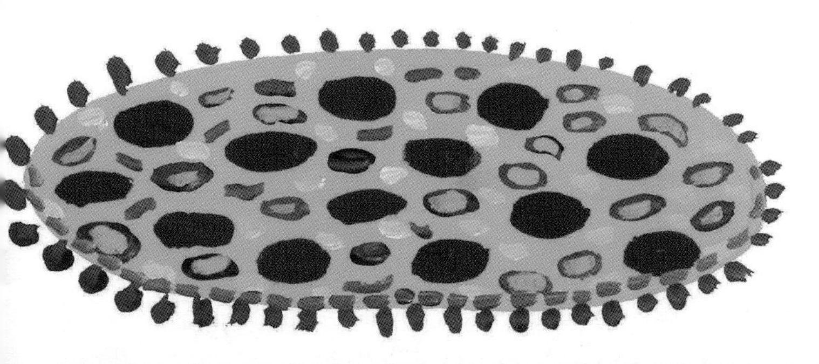

A Child's Prayer

Thank you God for sending me Jesus from above.

Please help me to be nice like Him and always share His love.

Thank you most, God, for loving me no matter what I do.

The Bible says You always love me. Now I know it's true.

Please help me God to grow to know you better each day.

Thank you God for watching over me while I learn and play.

Amen!

A Special Note for Parents

We designed this guide to help your angel come "alive" inside your hearts and home! Please encourage your child to find their angel on the pages of this book and in your home as she "reappears." We hope this book will become a new Christmas tradition that you begin reading each December 1st.

Please help your child look for the hidden Bible verses within this book. We designed the last page to include verses to be cut out to help your child learn God's Word.

Please read your child the following Scriptures as referenced in this book:

- Angel Gabriel appears to Mary with a special message, Luke 1:26-38
- The angel visits Joseph in a dream, Matthew 1:18-25
- The birth of Baby Jesus, Luke 2:1-20
- The Wise Men visit Baby Jesus, Matthew 2:9-11

Although her assignment ends Christmas Eve, her mission never ends! She sends year-round special biblical messages by way of Angel Mail, once you register her online at www.mysecretangelandme.com. Look for her as she "reappears" with each new message!

Have fun with your angel and teaching your child the true meaning of Christmas!

We pray your secret angel will be your child's lifelong friend and teacher.

How MY SECRET ANGEL AND ME Came to Be

Ashley and I are sisters-in-law, best friends and more importantly, sisters in Christ. The idea for this book came to Ashley one day as she was driving down the road with my inquisitive 4-year old nephew, Tyler Roo. Like most kids, he was anxious for Christmas and couldn't stop talking about all the presents he was getting from Santa.

Nearing a red light, Ashley heard a little voice inside her head ask, "How can you teach him the real meaning of Christmas?" She closed her eyes for a moment and that's when she saw her... our beautiful angel! Ashley knew her vision was sent straight from God! She imagined turning His vision into a "tangible" guardian angel doll that Tyler could connect with! The angel could tell the story of Jesus' birth and teach her son what Christmas is really all about! But there was one big fat red problem that just didn't fit with the Nativity. Santa Claus. Truth be told, celebrating the magic of Santa is fun for children, and she wanted to keep the magic alive. But how could she tie the angel, Jesus and Santa together? This is when I came in...

We were sitting together in our pajamas over Christmas talking about her "vision from God" and the idea to write a book. She is an amazing artist and I love to write, so we quickly agreed to collaborate on this project. Then all of a sudden, I got my sign from God. I looked at her square in the face and blurted out, "Here is something you never knew, God is the one who tells Santa what to do." We both got so excited! Yes, God is the boss of Santa! This was how we would spread the true meaning of Christmas to the world of gift loving children!

When Ashley first sent me her illustrations, I got the chills. And when I first shared my text, she cried! God clearly put the two of us together for a reason. We have felt led by "His" presence throughout this entire process. We hope your family will enjoy reading this book as much as we enjoyed creating it!

May God bless your family during this holiday season. Merry Christmas!

"This is the day that
the Lord has made;
Let us rejoice and be glad in it."
Psalm 118:24

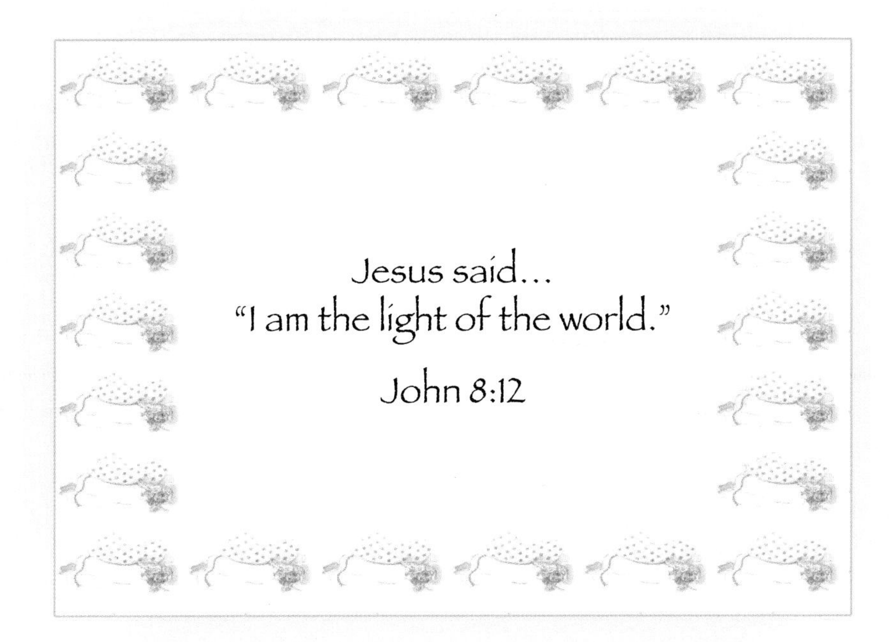
Jesus said...
"I am the light of the world."
John 8:12

"For he will command his angels
concerning you to guard you
in all your ways;"
Psalm 91:11

"...God is love."
1 John 4:8

A Letter from Your Secret Angel

Precious ones,

My name is special because you chose it just for me.
Please add it to the magic list called the Angel registry.

I'll send you special messages by way of *Angel Mail.*

I hope to stay in touch, my love for you will never fail!

Love,

____

Your Secret Angel and friend

www.mysecretangelandme.com - Official Angel Registry